USING THIS BOOK

One of the best ways of helping children to read, is by reading stories to them and with them.

*The first time you read this book, read the **whole** story to the child, looking at the illustrations together. Then, if the child is reading confidently, give him* the book to read on his own, whenever he wishes. If you think that more help is needed read the story again with him on another occasion, reading the left-hand pages yourself and asking him to read the right-hand pages. Build up his confidence by praise and encouragement as much as you can.*

*The child is referred to as 'he' in order to avoid the clumsy 'he or she', but the book is equally appropriate for girls and boys.

British Library Cataloguing in Publication Data

McCullagh, Sheila K.
  The magician's raindrops. — (Puddle Lane
  reading programme. Stage 5; v. 1)
  1. Readers — 1950-
  I. Title   II. Aitchison, Martin   III. Series
  428.6   PE1119

  ISBN 0-7214-1012-X

First edition

Published by Ladybird Books Ltd Loughborough Leicestershire UK
Ladybird Books Inc Lewiston Maine 04240 USA

© Text and layout SHEILA McCULLAGH MCMLXXXVII
© In publication LADYBIRD BOOKS LTD MCMLXXXVII

Printed in England

The Magician's raindrops

written by SHEILA McCULLAGH
illustrated by MARTIN AITCHISON

This book belongs to:

Ladybird Books

It was Saturday afternoon, and
Sarah and Davy were out in Puddle Lane.
They had made another wooden cart, and
they were having races down the lane.
They pulled the carts up to the gates
of the Magician's garden.
Then they turned them round, climbed in,
and raced back down the lane
to the post at the other end.

The first time they raced down,
Davy almost hit the post.
He pulled his cart to one side
just in time.

They had raced down the lane ten times,
and they had each won five races,
when Mrs Pitter-Patter opened her
front door and looked out.
"Sarah! Davy!" she cried, as they shot past.
"You're making too much noise.
Go home and help your mother."
Sarah skidded to a stop.
"She doesn't need any help,
Mrs Pitter-Patter," she said.
"She told us to come out
and play in the lane."
"Well, I'm sure your mother didn't mean
you to rush up and down like this,"
said Mrs Pitter-Patter.

"She doesn't mind," said Sarah.

"Well, I do," said Mrs Pitter-Patter.

"Go and play quietly somewhere else."
She shut her door.

"It **is** hot in the lane," said Davy,
coming back pulling his cart.
"Let's go into the Magician's garden."
"Let's go and see if we can see
any of those mice," said Sarah.
They left their carts at the garden gates,
and went into the garden.

They crept quietly across the grass,
and hid behind a bush
near the hollow tree,
to watch for the Wideawake Mice.

9

They didn't have to wait very long.
They had scarcely settled down,
when a little mouse came running along
through the grass, and looked down
the mousehole in the roots
of the hollow tree.
It was Hickory Mouse.
(Sarah and Davy didn't know his name,
but they could see he was a wood mouse,
because he had a white front
and a long tail.)
Hickory gave a loud squeak.

A few moments later, three other mice
came out of the hole to join him.
They began to play hide-and-seek
among the roots of the old tree.

Sarah and Davy had been watching the mice
for some time, when Davy heard
a faint sound behind him.
He looked round.
Tom Cat was creeping through the long grass.
He hadn't seen Sarah and Davy.
His eyes were on the mice.

Davy gripped Sarah's arm.

She turned, and saw Tom Cat.

Tom Cat crouched down, ready to spring.

"Scat!" cried Sarah, as loudly as she could.

"Look out!" cried Davy.

The little mice shot back down the mousehole.

Tom Cat's head jerked up.

He stared at Davy and Sarah.

"Scat!" cried Sarah again.

Davy waved his arm.

"Go away!" he shouted.

Tom Cat turned and ran back
to the gates. He crept under them,
and ran off down Puddle Lane.

"The mice will never be safe,
while that cat comes into the garden,"
said Sarah.
"Let's go and see the Magician,
and ask him to help us to stop
Tom Cat coming here," said Davy.

As they walked towards the big house,
the front door opened, and
the Magician came out.
"We were coming to see you," cried Sarah,
running up to him.
She told him all about Tom Cat.
"We don't want to hurt Tom Cat,"
said Davy. "But we want to keep him
away from the garden."
"I'll try and think of something,"
said the Magician. "But it may
take me a little time. But there is
something you could do for tonight,
if you would like to."
"We would," said Davy. "What is it?"

"I'll give you some magic raindrops,"
said the Magician.
"They will scare Tom Cat away,
and they won't hurt him.
Wait here. I'll go and get them."

The Magician went back into his house.
A few moments later, he came out again,
carrying a silver bowl.
He put it down on the steps.
Sarah and Davy looked in.
"It's only water," said Sarah.
She sounded very disappointed.
"It's only water now," said the Magician.
"But just wait a minute.
I'm going to make magic raindrops."

The Magician picked up the bowl again,
and held it in his hands.
He whispered something which Sarah and
Davy couldn't hear.
Then he put down the bowl again,
and snapped his fingers.

19

At once, the water began to bubble.
The bubbles floated up into the air,
until there was no water left
in the bowl.
Then, as Sarah and Davy watched,
each bubble dropped back
into the bowl again.
But the bubbles didn't break.
They lay there all together
in the bowl.
They looked like shining raindrops.

Soon, the bowl was full
of magic raindrops.
Each drop was about as big
as a pea.

The Magician picked up
one of the raindrops,
and held it between his fingers.
It had a long, silvery thread
hanging from it.
"Put these magic raindrops in the bushes
around the hollow tree, so that
the threads hang down," he said.
"If Tom Cat touches one of the threads,
it will stick to his fur and
the raindrop will break over his head.
He won't be able to get rid of it,
until he runs under the archway
out of Puddle Lane."
"The raindrops don't look very big,"
said Sarah.
"There isn't much water in them."

"There isn't much at the moment,"
said the Magician. "But they'll grow.
That's part of the magic.
They'll be as big as balloons,
before very long."

"What about the other animals in the garden?"
asked Davy. "Will they get wet, too?"
"Water won't hurt them," said the Magician.
"And the raindrops won't stick to them.
They will only stick to Tom Cat.
And the raindrops will only last
for one night.
They'll be gone in the morning."
The Magician gave the bowl to Sarah,
and went back into the house.

Sarah and Davy looked in the bowl.

"The raindrops are getting bigger already,"
said Sarah.

"At least they'll give Tom Cat
a bit of a shock," said Davy.

"Come on. Let's put them in the bushes."

Sarah and Davy took the raindrops,
and hid them in the bushes
all around the hollow tree.
No matter how high they put them,
the silvery threads hung down until
they almost touched the ground.
By the time the bushes were full
of magic raindrops, the drops
were almost as big as tennis balls.

"Let's put some in the trees, too,"
said Sarah. "Tom Cat will never see them,
if they're up in the trees."
Sarah and Davy reached up
as high as they could, and
hid some of the magic raindrops
in the branches of the trees.

"Let's hide, and see what happens," said Davy.
But at that moment,
they heard their mother calling.
"We'll have to go home and have tea,"
said Sarah. "But we'll come back afterwards."
They ran back to Puddle Lane.

*   *   *

"You mustn't be out too long,"
said their mother, as they opened
the front door to go out again
after tea. "You must be back
before sunset."
"We will be," said Sarah.

As they went out into the lane,
the gate of the garden opened,
and Peter Tall came out.
He was wet from head to foot.
Water was running down his neck,
and dripping off the end of his nose.

"Peter!" cried Sarah. "Whatever happened?"

"I was getting some sticks for my fire,"
said Peter. "A great whoosh of water
broke over my head."

"I'm so sorry, Peter," said Sarah.

"Oh, I'm all right," said Peter.

"Last time I came into the garden,
I met a monster, who puffed out fire.
I had to jump into the lake.
I was much wetter then."

He went off into his house.

"He must have met the Gruffle,"
said Davy. "We never go in the garden
when the Gruffle is there."

"Well, be careful you don't touch
the raindrops this time," said Sarah.
"You saw how wet Peter was."

They went into the garden,
and across to the hollow tree.
"They are as big as balloons!" cried Davy,
looking at one of the raindrops.

"Let's watch what happens next,"
said Sarah.
They hid behind a bush
near the hollow tree.
They hadn't been there long, when
they heard the gates of the garden open.
Sarah looked round the bush.
"It's the Gruffle!" she whispered.

The Gruffle went over to the house,
and after a minute or two,
they heard him scrunching something.
(He was eating some bits of coal
which the Magician had left outside
for him.)
"He's coming this way!" whispered Davy.

The Gruffle came over towards them
breathing out little puffs of smoke,
and grunting to himself.
As they watched, he moved under
the hollow tree –
and touched a thread of rain!

The great raindrop burst
over the Gruffle's head.
The Gruffle gave a loud roar.
Flames shot out of his mouth.
His head was hidden
in a cloud of steam.
He gave another roar, and vanished.

Sarah and Davy saw the cloud of steam
move towards the gates, and disappear
into Puddle Lane.

"Everybody seems to be getting wet
except Tom Cat," said Sarah.

"I'm sorry about the Gruffle," said Davy.

"He's afraid of mice. He wouldn't hurt them!"

"But he did look funny," said Sarah.

"I wonder who the next one will be."

"I hope it's Tom Cat," said Davy.

They waited, keeping very still.
The shadows in the garden grew longer.
"We shall have to go home soon,"
whispered Sarah.
"Sh!" breathed Davy. "Look!"
The little dragon had flown onto
a branch of the hollow tree.
He was looking down at the mousehole
in the roots.

As they watched, a little brown head
looked out of the hole.
It was Hickory.
He looked all around, but
he didn't look up into the tree.
The little dragon lifted his wings
ready to fly.
Hickory came right out of the hole.

As Sarah and Davy shouted a warning,
the little dragon hurled himself down
towards Hickory.
His right wing touched a rain thread.
The water from the magic drop
crashed onto his head,
knocking him to the ground.

For one second, Hickory
was too frightened to move.
Then he shot down the mousehole,
back under the hollow tree.

The little dragon picked himself up,
and flew up into the air.
He tried to shoot fire out of his mouth
as he flew past Davy and Sarah,
but he only managed a hiss of steam.
He disappeared down Puddle Lane.
"The mice won't come out again now,"
said Sarah. "And it's getting late.
We must go home.
I'm sorry that Tom Cat didn't come."

"I'm glad that the raindrop
hit the little dragon," said Davy.
"That was even better
than hitting Tom Cat."

Sarah and Davy were upstairs
getting ready for bed, when they heard
a fearful howl outside in Puddle Lane.
They ran to a window, and looked out.
Tom Cat was running down Puddle Lane
as fast as he could run.
He was dripping with water, and
he was pulling a giant raindrop
behind him.
The thread of rain was round his neck,
and the raindrop was floating
in the air, over his head.

Water was pouring down from it,
as Tom Cat ran along.
The water poured down –
but the raindrop didn't seem
to be getting any smaller.

Tom Cat disappeared down the lane,
howling as he went.

"Poor old Tom Cat," said Davy.
"He must have got a shock."

"He must have been after the mice,"
said Sarah. "The water won't hurt him.
The Magician said so. He's only wet.
And the raindrop will fall off
at the end of the lane."

"The Magician's raindrops really are magic,"
said Davy. "I don't think Tom Cat
will go after the mice again.
But I hope no one else gets wet."

"The raindrops will be gone by the morning,"
said Sarah.

Sarah and Davy turned away
from the window,
and went off to bed.

If you have enjoyed this longer story, here is another one for you to read:

Stage 5

2 **A dragon in the mountains**

This is the story about Irun and Sandella and other characters who live in the magical Country of Zorn.

Irun, Sandella and the quorn

The fire-breathing dragon

The Magician sends a messenger to help the children when the City of Zorn is in great danger from a fire-breathing dragon who comes down from the mountains.

There are five stories which tell you how Irun and Sandella came from Candletown to the Country of Zorn.

Stage 4
1 **When the clock struck thirteen**
tells you how the iron boy came to the Country of Zorn.

2 **The sandalwood girl**
is the story of what happened to a girl, carved out of wood, who was in the attic of the old house when the clock struck thirteen.

The story of the iron boy continues in
3 **On the way to the Blue Mountains**
which tells you about the adventures of the iron boy and the sandalwood girl, as they go on their dangerous journey.

4 **Fire in the grass**
continues their adventures.

5 **The Silver River**
tells of how the children are carried to the Blue Mountains by the silver ponies. When the boy and girl have bathed in the river, they become like ordinary children and finally meet someone who tells them their names.

from Fire in the grass

51